UNKILLABLE

A NICK LAWRENCE SHORT STORY

BRIAN SHEA

SEVERN RIVER PUBLISHING

Severn River Publishing
www.SevernRiverBooks.com

This is a work of fiction. Names, characters, businesses, places, events and incidents are either the products of the author's imagination or used in a fictitious manner. Any resemblance to actual persons, living or dead, or actual events is purely coincidental.

ISBN: 978-1-951249-33-5 (Paperback)

ALSO BY BRIAN SHEA

The Nick Lawrence Series

Kill List

Pursuit of Justice

Burning Truth

Targeted Violence

Murder 8

The Boston Crime Thriller Series

Murder Board

Bleeding Blue

The Penitent One

Sign of the Maker

Cold Hard Truth

The Sterling Gray FBI Profiler Series

Hunting the Mirror Man

The King Snake

The Butcher of Belarus

The Green Samurai

To find out more, visit

severnriverbooks.com/authors/brian-shea

To the ones that didn't come back home.

UNKILLABLE

The wind rattled against the metal walls of the refurbished container, his home away from home. Sand and small bits of rock accompanied the gust adding a melodic ringing, like rain on a farmer's tin roof, Nick Lawrence lay on his cot. His feet crested the edge at the ankles, and he'd placed a rolled wool blanket underneath to adjust for the discomfort. Eyes closed but not asleep, Nick absorbed this moment of peace. He seized every opportunity to find the serenity in his current surroundings, and he deemed these desert storms to be the optimal condition.

A deafening rumble shattered the tranquility. The sound, like a wildebeest in heat, shook the walls. Nick's eyes shot open.

"Mother of God, Grant!" Nick yelled as he threw a half-eaten box of graham crackers at his roommate.

The box founds its mark, striking Sergeant Grant Sellers on his forehead. The impact of the lightweight cardboard was enough to rip him from his laborious slumber.

"What the—?" Sellers muttered as he sat up. The thin

frame of the smaller stature Sellers barely gave the olive drab frame of the cot cause to squeak.

"For such a small guy, you sure as hell make a lot of racket," Nick said.

"My wife complained every night. Now she misses it. Just like you'll miss it when we go back home," Sellers said with a chuckle, digging his hand into the box that struck him. He shoved the square, sugar-coated cracker into his mouth, sending a shower of crumbs onto his beige t-shirt.

"I seriously doubt that," Nick retorted and looked down at his watch: 19:47 hours.

The two had gone through this same repartee more times than Nick could recall since they'd arrived in Afghanistan seven months ago. Other members of their unit referred to them as the "odd couple." Nick, always calm and collected, while his counterpart was a loud, hot mess. Under fire, both men had proven their worth, and the two had become inseparable. But their separation was inevitable. Sellers only had three months left in his enlistment and would soon be returning to civilian life. Nick still had over a year and half left in his obligation. That was the way of things, but the thought of entering the battlefield without Sellers saddened him and he pushed the thought from his mind.

A loud rap on the door interrupted their banter.

Nick sauntered to the door and unlatched it, opening it to the nervous sway of Private First Class Dietrich. He was new to the unit, having arrived only three weeks before. The gangly teenager—only nineteen—stood before Nick, his pale face was blotched with nerves. Others took great pride in messing with the new guys, but Nick found no pleasure in those types of games.

Nick gave a welcoming smile but said nothing. Dietrich

fidgeted awkwardly as he prepared to speak the words he had most likely rehearsed a hundred times before knocking.

"Lieutenant Lawrence, your presence is requested by Colonel Granfield in the TOC," Dietrich said, sounding winded from the effort.

"When?" Nick asked.

"Now, sir," Dietrich said bashfully.

"Tell the Colonel I'm on my way," Nick said, turning away from the young private and closing the door.

Nick walked back to his cot and sat. He laced his boots and could feel Sellers eyeing him. Nick waited for his friend to speak.

"What do you think this is all about?" Sellers said, percolating with interest.

"I have no idea. I'll find out soon enough," Nick said, rolling his eyes. He knew Sellers was already creating an endless list of possibilities. Although it happened infrequently, every time Nick had been called in to see the Battalion Commander, Sellers became overly excited. Most times, the fanfare was ill deserved, and it was usually an administrative tasking.

Nick threw on his fatigue top and fitted his patrol cap on his head, tightening the Ranger roll before stepping out into the hallway of their makeshift barracks.

* * *

The wind spewed bits of sand against Nick's outstretched left palm as he shielded his face from the barrage. He moved out from the alleyway formed by the rowed container units of his living quarters and into the open space of the forward operating base. This was an unforgiving place. Nick set a quick pace, knowing it was never good to keep his commander waiting.

The Tactical Operations Center, or TOC, blended into the surrounding structures scattered around the base. The exterior of the building was covered in weather-beaten plywood. The rationale was simple: minimize exposure and blend. An ops center was useless if the enemy could immediately recognize its significance.

Dietrich stood outside. A small awning projecting out from the entrance sheltered his body from sandblasting winds. At the sight of Nick, the youthful private snapped to attention and brought his hand up in salute with the tips of his pointer and middle finger contacting the bent brim of his patrol cap. "Rangers lead the way, sir!" Dietrich belted.

"All the way!" Nick said, giving the standard response while simultaneously returning the salute. Nick understood the formality of rank, but never let his position of leadership go to his head. On the battlefield rank meant little when the rounds flew. He never took for granted any man who took up arms beside him. To Nick, all were his brothers.

Nick gave Dietrich a nod, stepped past him, and into the confines of the TOC. The interior walls were a combination of reinforced steel beams and poured concrete. It would hold up against a small-scale enemy attack. Normally the space buzzed with the chatter of Intel and Ops guys, but this evening it was uncannily quiet. Colonel Granfield stood with his back to the door and did not turn at the sound of Nick's entrance. He appeared to be engaged in conversation, but from Nick's angle he couldn't see with whom.

"Lieutenant Lawrence, reporting as ordered, sir!" Nick announced. He was the one now standing at attention. His body rigid and his thumb pressed into the crux of his pointer finger's folded position, running along the line of his fatigues' seam. His turn to be the subordinate.

"At ease," the Colonel said with a thick Boston accent. Colonel Granfield's humble beginnings in the south end of the city, affectionately known as "Southie", never left the man over the course of his twenty years of military service. Nick recalled how his commanding officer would drop the ability to properly pronounce an *r* once he had a couple pints in him.

"Yes sir," Nick said, instantaneously releasing the tension in his shoulders.

"Nick, come on over here. I'd like you to meet someone," Granfield said. The Colonel stepped aside, giving Nick a clear visual of the person his commanding officer had been speaking with. The man casually sitting at one of the nearby consoles looked to be in his late twenties or early thirties. He had short, jet-black hair longer than military regulations would allow, which immediately told Nick he must either be a contractor or more likely a spook. The CIA would occasionally drop in a person to provide a pre-mission intelligence briefing.

Nick crossed the space, navigating around the computers and work stations littering the tight area. Colonel Granfield reached out a hand and Nick shook it. The seated man stood and also shook Nick's hand. The man had a strong grip, but not so much that he was trying to prove a level of toughness. It seemed to be a natural demonstration of the man's strength.

"Nick, this is Jay. He's here on some business, and we will be providing him with some support," Granfield said.

"Let me know what you need me to do," Nick said.

"I'm going to let Jay brief you," Granfield said, taking a slight step back to allow Jay to assert himself.

"Your Colonel tells me you're one hell of a leader on the battlefield," Jay said.

Nick found himself uncomfortable with compliments. He'd always shied away from the spotlight. "Thanks," he muttered awkwardly.

"I'm not really here. And what we're going to be doing tomorrow is classified. I'm limited in what I can tell you, but the long and short of it is you'll be providing me with ground level fire support during a meet and greet. It's a deal I've brokered and has been a long time in the coming," Jay said.

"Okay, how big of an element are we putting together for this?" Nick asked.

"Four," Jay responded.

"Nick, pick your best three. I trust your judgment, and I'm leaving this to you," Granfield chimed in.

Nick didn't answer but gave a solemn nod in response. This was a test of his leadership. The hand picking of a team where the end result could be death was one of the heaviest decisions any leader could face. He would not take this lightly.

Jay turned and manipulated the mouse on the computer behind him and a satellite image appeared on the screen. "This is where we're going. Not too far from here, but more importantly it's close enough to the Pakistani border that my connection feels comfortable with the meet."

Nick peered over Jay's shoulder and looked at the expanse of rugged topography. It all looked the same. Poorly constructed roads cut through the zigzag of mountains littering the countryside. A couple clicks of the keyboard and the screen zoomed in, displaying a dirt pathway leading from the main road. A few small dwellings were scattered along like dying leaves hanging onto a branch in winter.

"Three homes. A farmer and his family live there. Intel claims it's neutral territory. But this is Afghanistan and nothing's ever a guarantee. And that's where you and your team come in. My contact should have a small security detail, and I want one too," Jay said. He was calm, and Nick surmised Jay had done similar operations in the past.

Nick stared at the image on the screen, committing it to memory. "When do we leave?"

"We'll meet up here at 0400 hours. I want to head out before the base is in full swing. Plus, we've got a little drive ahead of us, and I like to move under the cover of darkness," Jay answered.

"What about support?" Nick asked with a trace of concern.

"I've got that end of it, Nick. We'll have two helos from the 160th standing by for an extract or additional fire support if the need dictates," Granfield said, rejoining the conversation.

"Sounds good," Nick said. "I'll have my team standing by and ready to go at 0400."

"Strip it down for tomorrow," Jay said.

Nick cocked his head in slight confusion at the lingo. "Strip it down?"

"No name tags, patches, or dog tags," Jay said.

Nick felt a prickle along his neck. Suddenly this mission felt more complicated. He exhaled the tension and nodded. "Anything else before I go brief my guys?"

"Not on my end. See you in the morning," Jay said.

"Good luck tomorrow, son," Granfield said.

"I won't let you down," Nick said.

"You haven't so far," Granfield said, giving Nick a hearty slap on his back.

Nick exited the same door he'd entered. Dietrich still stood by outside, manning his post. Nick flashed an absent-minded salute as his thoughts shifted to the task of selecting the members of his team.

* * *

He cranked the handle to his cargo hold of a room. There was no way to enter these quarters silently and the clang of metal on metal as the latch released noisily announced his arrival. Sellers sat up from his supine position on his cot and eagerly stared at Nick.

Nick chuckled at the sight of his friend. "Jesus, Grant, if you had a tail it'd be wagging."

"Come over here and rub my belly," Grant said, rolling onto his back, bending his arms and legs, and panting loudly with his tongue out in a pathetic performance.

Nick walked past his friend and tossed his hat on the upturned milk crate he used as an end table.

Grant sat up. "Are you going to tell me about your private meeting with the Colonel or am I going to have to beg again?"

Nick paused, debating whether he wanted to watch his friend resume his animal charades. "Small unit mission."

"How small?" Sellers asked.

"Four."

"Who's going?" Sellers asked.

"That's the thing—I've been given total control on the team," Nick said.

Sellers rubbed his hands together and beamed. "Well, you only have to pick two more."

"I didn't say you were going," Nick said.

"You don't have to. You'd be lost without me," Sellers said.

Nick said nothing and plopped heavily into the cot. The springs rang out their pleas of resistance.

"Seriously? Why wouldn't you want me on this one?"

"It's not that—I got a bad feeling on this one," Nick said, casting his eyes downward.

"Don't give me that Spidey Sense crap! If you think it could break bad, then I definitely want to be there," Sellers said, giving a look that conveyed the seriousness of his statement.

"And there's nobody I'd rather have by my side than you, but—I don't think I could live with myself if I hand-picked you and something happened."

"I didn't join the Peace Corps. I joined the Army," Sellers said emphatically.

"I know."

Sellers rolled up his left sleeve and tapped the tattoo bent in an arc across his shoulders. The bright yellow letters set against the black background spelled out RANGER. "This is who I am and those that stand beside me are my brothers."

Nick knew what his friend was waiting to hear. They'd said these words to each other before every mission the two had gone on together. "I am my brother's keeper," Nick said, finishing his part in their mantra.

With that said, Nick had only two more members of his unit to select for the morning's mission. He felt the burdensome weight of leadership resting squarely on his broad shoulders.

"So, any ideas on who else is coming to the party?" Sellers asked.

Nick rubbed his temples. "Blier and Wolcott."

"Good choices. Blier's a bit green, but he makes good decisions under duress," Sellers said, validating Nick's decision.

With Sellers onboard, Nick felt the worrisome load of the mission lift slightly. He set out with Sellers to brief his hand-picked team.

Once the rest of his team was brought up to speed Nick and Sellers returned to their room. Sellers was asleep as soon as his head hit the pillow. Nick closed his eyes, attempting to relax his restless mind for the few hours he had left before the start of the mission.

* * *

Every letter Nick had received from friends and family back stateside had always asked him about the weather. Their assumption was that it was desert hot all the time. Their assessment couldn't be further from the truth. The Connecticut winters of his childhood had nothing on the climate he'd experienced overseas. The cold dry air of the early morning stung his face and burned his lungs with the first few inhales as he walked with Sellers toward the TOC. There was no Dietrich standing guard now. Instead Blier and Wolcott were huddled by the entrance.

"Good morning sir," Blier said as he readied himself for a salute.

"Save it. No rank today," Nick said, smiling and patting the empty fuzz in the center of his chest, where his Velcro rank patch would have normally been attached.

"So, where's the spook?" Wolcott asked. He and Blier stood about the same height, but Wolcott was the larger man by almost seventy pounds. He looked more like a professional linebacker than the typical wiry frame of most of the other men in the unit.

"Boo!" Jay said, stepping from the around the plywood corner of the building. Jay wore jeans and a black, long-sleeved coat over a tactical vest.

"This is Sellers, Blier, and Wolcott. A good group to have if things go bad," Nick said, in a fanning gesture identifying each individual soldier as he said their names.

With small talk and introductions out the way, Jay pointed them toward their transport. It was a dark blue Jeep Cherokee that looked like someone had rolled it down a mountain before it showed up in the motor pool. Dents and dirt covered every bit of the vehicle's exterior.

"No Hummer?" Sellers asked.

"Trust me. She's ugly, but one hell of a good ride," Jay said.

"You just described Blier's girlfriend," Wolcott jested. Blier gave him an obligatory shove.

"Well, look who's volunteered to drive," Nick said. He'd already told Wolcott he'd be the driver, but felt it was a good time to remind him.

Nick pulled the back door open and immediately saw why Jay liked the Jeep.

"Reinforced frame. The windows and side paneling in the doors are bulletproofed. They're rated to withstand up to five rounds of 7.62mm ball ammunition before failure. It's also got run-flat tires," Jay said.

"Best part is these seats!" Sellers said, bouncing up and down in the seat like a kid getting ready to go to the zoo. Unlike the uncomfortable Hummer, these seats looked as though they'd been plucked from a BMW.

Nick sat on the passenger side behind Jay, accompanied by Sellers and Blier. Wolcott pulled out onto the dirt road leading out of the base.

"So, do you have any connections in the FBI?" Sellers asked loudly, competing with the roar of the engine.

"Oh God, here he goes again," Blier said, shaking his head. He leaned forward, directing his attention to Jay. "Sorry buddy, but anytime Sellers here meets anybody from a three-letter agency, he asks about the FBI. Some childhood dream of his."

Nick noticed Sellers reddened slightly at the chastisement but that he didn't cower. "Seriously, I'm almost done with my time here and looking for an in with the Bureau."

"I could probably put you in touch with some people. Mind me asking why the Bureau?" Jay asked sincerely.

"My dad is a cop, back in Albuquerque. He said he always wanted to be an agent, but he didn't meet the degree requirements. I come from a long line of law enforcement, but I'm the first to graduate college. So, I guess I'm fulfilling my dad's dream," Sellers said, giving the same speech he'd given numerous times in the past.

"That's an honorable reason. After we get back from this meeting today, I'll get your info and reach out to some people who owe me a favor or two. No promises, but I'll do what I can," Jay said.

Nick never tired of hearing his friend's reasoning in becoming an agent. The passion in his voice was contagious. He wished that he had a plan for life after the military, but so far nothing seemed to stick.

They filled the remaining two hours with Sellers' mindless banter and the heavy snores of Blier who'd fallen asleep shortly after the Jeep cleared the base's walls. Blier's head now rested against the heavily padded shoulder straps of Nick's ballistic vest. Blier managed to remain sound asleep through every jostle of the vehicle as it passed over the underdeveloped third-world highway. Nick was jealous. Insomnia had struck shortly after his arrival in country and he considered himself lucky if he got four hours.

The Jeep slowed. "Heads up. We're about two minutes out," Jay called out.

Nick gave a hard nudge to the left. Blier sat up and quickly composed himself, wiping the drool from the corner of his mouth.

"Sleeping beauty's awake," Sellers said with a chuckle.

All three men in the back sat upright with the barrels of their M4's pointed down between their feet toward the floorboard. Without speaking each man toggled the selector switch to semi. Unlike the movies, a jacketed 5.56mm round was already chambered and ready. The jovial nature of the conversation ceased, and each man registered the seriousness of their arrival. Nick eyed each of his hand-picked teammates and was confident he'd selected the right men.

Wolcott veered the Jeep onto the branched dirt road that Jay had shown Nick during their meeting. Nick compared the layout he'd committed to memory from the satellite imagery he'd seen and was impressed at its accuracy.

Jay pointed to the largest of the three structures, set in the middle of a semicircle of clay huts atop the crest of the small hill. "That's the one over there."

As soon as the vehicle stopped, Sellers and Nick hopped out, quickly covering both sides of the vehicle as they scanned for threats with their rifles at the low ready.

"Clear left," Sellers said.

"Clear right," Nick said, and then conducted one more visual sweep. Satisfied, he announced, "All clear."

Hearing the all clear, the rest of the group stepped out. Jay moved toward the entrance of the home. The exterior was constructed of packed clay and matched the sepia of the surrounding landscape. Chipped red paint sparsely coated the metal door, indicative of the weathering of the harsh environmental conditions. Jay banged loudly two times and then stepped back from the door. Nick noticed that the CIA man rested his hand uneasily on the butt of the Glock protruding from the thigh rig strapped to his right leg.

The quiet was unnerving and then he heard a shuffling sound from the other side of the door accompanied by a muffled whisper. The sounds stopped, and the quiet returned. Then a clang and the door opened. In the threshold stood a thin man wearing a leather jacket over his more traditional

Pashtun clothing. His hair was short and styled, in contrast to most of the people Nick had encountered. The man's olive complexion was light, an indicator of his station in life. He most likely didn't toil in the fields or shepherd a flock. The man's dark eyes brightened at the sight of Jay and the two men gave a quick embrace. Jay turned and nodded.

Nick and his team moved closer. Jay turned to Nick and said in a hushed tone, "Have one standby outside by the Jeep."

Nick nodded and turned to Wolcott, who was bringing up the rear, "Hang loose out here. Stay frosty."

"Roger that," Wolcott said with no hint of annoyance at being tasked. Wolcott was good like that, further reaffirming Nick's decision in selecting the oversized Ranger.

"Welcome, my friends," the man in the leather coat said with a barely perceptible accent. A smile stretched broadly across the man's thin face and his arms opened in a friendly manner. He then stepped close to Jay, and slapped his shoulder.

"Good to see you again," Jay said.

Nick entered behind Jay. The host turned his attention to Nick, giving him a quick once over before extending his hand. "I'm Ali."

Nick shook his hand, "Patrick." Nick assumed that Ali was not this man's name, just as Jay was most likely not accurate either. Nick used his brother's name, showing he could play the same game. Jay must've caught this because he looked back over his shoulder and gave a half-smile.

Sellers and Blier closed out the entry. The small hut was bigger on the inside than Nick had previously guessed from the outside. The group navigated a narrow hallway, and he counted three doors. They passed two closed doors staggered along the left side. The third door was on the right and was open. The sweet smell of ginger wafted out and greeted Nick's nostrils. He located the source once stepping inside. An ornate tea set was set on a wood table against the back wall. The steam from the freshly brewed tea danced from the pot, its tendrils swaying wildly in the cool air.

More interesting than the tea was the large man standing next to the table. He was Nick's height, but definitely had a few pounds on him and from the looks of it, most was muscle. The loose-fitting garb did little to mask the thick rounded shoulders and biceps laying underneath. This man stood in contrast to the jovial Ali. The bodyguard's beard was thick and long, ending at the sternum. This was a man of violence. Nick knew this looking at the twisted shape of the man's nose, obviously broken and rebroken several times over the man's life. Nick assumed it made sense Ali would have a personal bodyguard and protection detail. There was no visible weapon on the man, but that didn't mean he didn't have one. Nick's concern shifted to how many more men were scattered among those closed doors.

"I'm sorry it's not warmer, but tea always helps," Ali said.

"I'll take a cup," Jay said, accepting the invitation.

Ali gestured toward Nick and his team and nodded at the tea. "Gentlemen, may I offer you some Khawah?"

Nick gave a polite smile and shook his head. Sellers and Blier followed suit. Nick's role was security and he would be useless holding a cup of tea. Nick slipped off to the right and posted along the nearest corner. Sellers did the same on the other side and Blier stood aside but held his position by the door.

Ali nodded to the big man. Nick's grip tightened on his weapon, still resting at the low ready. The bodyguard nimbly picked up a bell resting on the table. The bell looked tiny is his large hand. He gave it a firm shake and the clapper ball banged against the casting, sending out a loud chime.

A door in the hallway opened and closed followed the by the shuffle of approaching footsteps. In the threshold a boy of maybe twelve appeared. He was very clean for the conditions of these quarters and Nick assumed the boy also probably traveled with Ali. The boy gave a slight bow of his head in the direction of Ali who smiled in return, holding up two fingers. The boy then scurried across the floor to the table along the back wall and began pouring the tea. The bodyguard did not move and did not look down at the boy. His gaze was focused on Ali and Jay.

The boy gingerly approached, and the porcelain cups rattled against the tray with each step. The boy served Jay first as was customary. Nick watched as Jay accepted the hot beverage. The boy then moved closer to Ali and offered up the remaining cup. Ali smiled and slipped his finger through the cup's handle and retrieved it from the tray. The boy remained standing, and Nick watched as Ali gave the boy a gentle pat on the back. Ali's hand then slid down the boy's spine and came to rest just above the child's buttocks. Nick noted Ali's hand and the awkward smile at the boy's attempt to feign acceptance. In that moment Nick saw the perversion of the man at the center of this important meeting, and the thought sickened him.

Either Jay didn't notice or chose to ignore the subtle gesture, but the two men continued their quiet conversation without missing a step. Nick couldn't make out what they were saying, but the two were whispering in rapid-fire succession only pausing long enough to sip from the tea in hand.

Ali's hand retreated, and the boy took his empty tray to the table and began quietly organizing the arrangement of cups and spoons.

Nick saw a flash of anger wash over Jay. Ali responded by giving a reassuring smile, but at the corner of his eye there was a glimmer of satisfaction. Something wasn't right, but without knowing why they were there and what was being said, he had no idea exactly what was wrong.

"Months! You and I have been working on this for months!" Jay's voice broke the hushed tones of the conversation.

"Relax, my friend. There is no reason for you to raise your voice. This is life. Some things don't go as we would like. You of all people should understand that," Ali said. His voice was louder, but not quite reaching the level of Jay's.

"Those weapons are already on the move. You can't change who they go to at the last minute!" Jay yelled.

"What do you care? Your country has been putting weapons in the wrong hands for years. I'm just fixing your mistake. You should be thanking me," Ali said, giving an antagonistic smile.

"The deal is off! I'm shutting it down," Jay said, taking a step back from Ali. Nick watched as the friendly posturing of moments ago was replaced with a palpable animosity.

"That's where you are again wrong," Ali said, casting a quick glance at his bodyguard as he took a sip of his tea.

The large man moved deftly, launching himself from the wall with an impressive speed. He covered the short distance before Nick could take a shot. The large man kicked the back of Jay's legs sending the CIA operative backward while simultaneously snaking a large arm around his throat. Jay's arm was pinned by his side making it impossible to withdraw his sidearm. Nick angled his weapon up, and he could see Blier and Sellers holding fast at the same position. Jay's writhing body shielded any clear shot for Nick and his team.

"Let him go, and we all walk out of here!" Nick boomed.

"I don't think so," Ali said, taking a step and disappearing behind the large frame of his bodyguard.

Jay's left hand was free and fought wildly to relieve the constricting pressure of the large man's forearm. A bang of doors from out in the hallway. Nick's eyes widened at confirmation of his earlier fear. Gunfire erupted, ripping through the clay walls of the small room. Nick's aim was interrupted. It felt as though he'd been punched in the back of his left shoulder. The impact spun him to the right.

Nick looked over toward the door and saw Blier was face down, unmoving in a pool of blood. Sellers had turned his weapon on the approaching threat. He was sending rounds back through the walls blindly returning fire at the unseen enemy. Nick shook off the dizziness from the round that had struck—focused his mind. Get Blier! Nick fired three-round bursts with each step as he moved quickly toward the threshold of the door where Blier's body lay.

"Blier!" Nick shouted above the gunfire, hoping he was down but not out. Nothing in return. Nick pulled a grenade, releasing the pin, and button hooked it down the hallway without looking. "Frag out!" He yelled. Nick then grabbed Blier by the strap of his vest, using his right arm to pull him. His left arm was useless and swung loosely while he dragged Blier's body across the dirt floor. The blood smeared a dark trail as Nick pulled him back to the corner.

He ran his finger along the neck line of his fallen team mate. Blier had no discernible pulse. The concussion of the grenade shook the foundation of the poorly constructed farmhouse, toppling the wall behind Nick. Screams rained out, but Sellers silenced them with bursts from his M4.

The men in the hallway weren't firing anymore, and Nick turned his attention back to the center of the room. He was on the ground next to Blier's lifeless body, and he brought his rifle up to take aim on Ali and his bodyguard. Nick watched as Jay continued his losing fight for oxygen. Nick took a lower point of aim and fired. The first struck the ground, but the second found its mark striking the big man the ankle. The bullet had a crippling effect on the mountainous bodyguard, instantly causing him to release Jay from the choke hold.

Jay spun away and fell backward, withdrawing the Glock from his thigh rig and firing into the large man's chest until the slide locked to the rear. The young boy stood frozen in horror and his once clean face was painted in the deep red of the bodyguard's blood. Jay dropped the magazine from the now empty gun.

"No!" Sellers yelled from his corner.

Nick turned to see his best friend's head rock back as a deafening shot reverberated. Nick switched his attention back toward the center of the room. His mind was reeling to catch up. Ali stood with the heel of his soft leather shoe pressing down on Jay's gun hand. His pistol moved from the fatal shot delivered to Sellers, and he leveled at the CIA operative's head.

Nick angled his rifle at Ali, using his knee for balance. He pulled the trigger. Click.

Ali redirected his attention to Nick and fired two rounds from the pistol in his hand. The impact struck Nick's left shoulder in succession, the same area of his shoulder where he'd already taken one round. It knocked him back, and the torque toppled him atop the dead body of Blier.

"You and I are walking out of here. What happens down the road will depend on your cooperation," Ali said, with a calm that was in stark contradiction to the calamity of the situation.

"Might as well end it here then," Jay said, spitting the words.

"Bravery is wasted on men like the ones you brought here with you. Do you see the end result of their valor? Men like you and I see the bigger picture. In time, I'm sure you'll come around," Ali said.

"I hope you can run really fast, because I called in an air strike when your big dead friend was choking the life out of me," Jay said, looking down at his waistline.

Ali gestured with the gun for Jay to show him. With his free hand Jay pulled up to reveal a little black box clipped to his belt. It looked like a pager and the screen had a red flashing light. It was a targeting beacon and Ali's face darkened in anger.

"You're a stupid man," Ali hissed.

A roar, like that of a wild boar trapped in a hunter's snare, filled the room. Ali looked in the direction of the noisy interruption. A visceral rage danced across Nick's face as he ran head down and eyes up. The blood and dirt mixed, creating a macabre mask and giving Nick a savage look. He gripped the Ka-Bar tightly with his right arm coiled.

Nick covered the fourteen feet separating him from the man responsible for killing his team and best friend before Ali's brain could react to the attack. Nick drove all seven inches of the black-coated steel blade into the left temple of his enemy. The force of Nick's momentous charge caused both men to tumble wildly into a tangled heap on the ground. Nick righted himself atop the man, preparing to deliver another blow but realized his initial strike had neutralized his target. He smelled the leather from the coat as he pushed himself off the dead man.

Jay sat up and patted Nick on the shoulder. "Thank you," he wheezed.

Nick looked back over his shoulder but said nothing. His eyes were still filled with the anger coursing through his veins.

"We've got to go," Jay said, slapping a spare magazine into his Glock and racking the slide forward.

"I've got to get my men," Nick said, devoid of emotion.

"Air strike is inbound. That wasn't a bluff," Jay said.

"You called in a strike package on our location?" Nick said, fury percolating just beneath the surface.

"Listen, we don't have time to debate my op planning with a chopper inbound with a Hellfire missile package. We don't want to be here when it arrives!" Jay said desperately. "This a one-way transmitter. A failsafe if things took a turn."

Jay clasped Nick's right forearm and pulled him up. Nick retrieved his M4, and Jay helped seat a fresh thirty-round magazine for him. Nick followed Jay's lead out through the rubble of the hallway. The mangled bodies of Ali's assault team littered the walk. There was no movement and no sound except the crunch of their boots on the jagged bits of rock and rebar.

Nick stepped out the door they had been welcomed through only twenty minutes before and looked over toward the Jeep. He could see the twisted sole of Wolcott's boot peeking out from the behind the rear tire and knew without a doubt that the big soldier was dead.

In the quiet stillness, Nick's heart sank as he absorbed the thought of his dead friends.

"Time's a-ticking," Jay said, looking down at the black box on his hip. In the distance, the familiar thumping of a helicopter on approach could be heard

Nick ignored Jay's comment and walked to the back of the Jeep. He hoisted Wolcott's heavy body into a seated position. Wolcott was surrounded by a of sea of spent brass casings. The sight of it gave Nick solace to know his Ranger went down fighting.

Jay assisted Nick in hoisting the big-framed Wolcott into the back seat of the Jeep. Jay jumped into the driver's seat.

Nick walked past the seated CIA operative and back toward the decimated farmhouse.

"What the hell are you doing?" Jay hollered.

"Getting my soldiers. They're not going to be buried here today!" Nick shouted without looking back.

Nick pulled Blier by his straps. His strength waned as the rubble snagged and pulled at Blier's uniform. Jay appeared in the doorway.

"I've got him. Hurry," Jay said.

Nick burst back into the room containing his best friend. He bent down and pulled him up on his shoulder. The lifeless body of his friend was heavier than he looked and Nick strained to stand. He heard quiet sobbing and turned to see the servant boy bent over the body of Ali.

"You should go. This house is coming down," Nick said. The boy's eyes flashed with anger and then returned to the fallen Ali.

Nick stumbled out through the hallway and into the light of day. Jay rushed to him, panic in his eyes. Jay unclipped the box from his belt. The red dot continued its rhythmic flashing. Jay hurled the box into the open dilapidated red door of the house.

Jay hopped into the driver's seat, and Nick took the passenger side. Jay whipped the steering wheel hard and pressed on the accelerator. The Jeep kicked up rocks and the heavy vehicle fishtailed as they pulled out onto the main roadway, leaving a swirling wake of dust.

Nick slumped in the seat. Absent the adrenaline dump, the blood loss took its toll and he felt the strength drain from his body. He slumped in his seat and watched the hillside erupt in bright orange flames as the Hellfire found its mark. The Jeep shook violently, indicating its proximity to the blast. Nick's eyes fluttered and closed to darkness.

* * *

Nick slowly sat up in the sterile environment of the forward operating base's medical facility. The IV connected to his right arm dripped slowly. He looked down at the thick block of padded gauze that bulged around his left shoulder. His left arm, immobilized in a sling, throbbed in a muted reminder of the trauma. The pain was mitigated by medication intravenously being fed to him.

The curtain swung wide and Jay appeared. Nick stared at him, unsure of his feelings toward the man. He didn't blame him for the deaths of his team. This was war and the small battles needed to be fought, even if the point and purpose weren't fully understood. He knew Jay had a job to do and Nick's team died supporting it. He just hoped that whatever the mission's overall objective had been, it was worth the lives of Sellers, Blier, and Wolcott.

"I'm sorry about your team," Jay said earnestly.

Nick said nothing.

"You did a hell of thing back there," Jay said.

Nick let his silence speak for him. *Hell of a thing, getting my team killed?*

"Going back for your fallen soldiers after being shot. Not many would do what you did," Jay said.

"No way I was going to let that place be their grave," Nick said softly.

"I'd be dead too if it wasn't for you. Two of those rounds in your chest were meant for me," Jay said.

"Do you want them back?" Nick asked in a feeble attempt at humor.

Jay paused, and then withdrew a business card from his pocket. "Your friend, Sellers, had asked me about connections in the Bureau. Not sure that's something you're interested in too, but I'd be more than willing to pay that favor forward."

Nick took the card. It was blank except for a phone number. "I'll think about it."

"My offer to you never expires."

"Thanks," Nick said.

Nick flicked the card onto the nightstand next to his bed, not realizing at the time how important Jay's connection would later prove to be.

Jay turned to leave and stopped, looking back at Nick. "Craziest thing I've ever seen, watching you run at him. I guess you proved wrong the age old saying about bringing a knife to a gun fight."

Nick made his best attempt at a smile.

"You're one unkillable son of a bitch."

KILL LIST

TO STOP A TERRORIST ATTACK, A VETERAN FBI AGENT MUST JOIN FORCES WITH A BANK ROBBER.

"...quick-moving, exciting, and eventful..." —**Booklife Prize Critic's Report**

FBI Special Agent Nick Lawrence has just transferred to the bank robbery unit based out of Connecticut's New Haven field office. Near his breaking point after the recent death of his father, he makes the move to care for his aging mother.

Declan Enright, a former police officer recently fired over a controversial shooting, has reached his own breaking point. Confronted with insurmountable financial burdens in the wake of his early termination, Declan is desperate for a way to provide for his wife and three daughters. Tapping into an elite skill set forged during his time as a Navy special warfare operator, and using the insider knowledge of a former police officer, Declan crosses the threshold and commits the perfect crime.

Nick is assigned to the case, and begins closing in. But when a series of terrorist attacks rattles the nation, the two men find their fates intertwined.

And the only way to prevent the next attack is to work together...

BRIAN SHEA has served as both a military officer and law

enforcement Detective, and his authentic works of fiction have been enjoyed by thousands.

Get your copy today at
severnriverbooks.com/series/nick-lawrence

ABOUT THE AUTHOR

Brian Shea has spent most of his adult life in service to his country and local community. He honorably served as an officer in the U.S. Navy. In his civilian life, he reached the rank of Detective and accrued over eleven years of law enforcement experience between Texas and Connecticut. Somewhere in the mix he spent five years as a fifth-grade school teacher. Brian's myriad of life experience is woven into the tapestry of each character's design. He resides in New England and is blessed with an amazing wife and three beautiful daughters.

Sign up for the reader list at
severnriverbooks.com/authors/brian-shea

Printed in the United States
by Baker & Taylor Publisher Services